The Three Billy Goats Gruff

BASED ON A TRADITIONAL FOLK TALE

retold by Irene Yates ★ *illustrated by* Sam Childs

Once upon a time there were three billy goats Gruff, Gruff, Gruff, who said, "This grass isn't good enough! We need to look for pastures new, where the grass is sweet and delicious to chew."

Off they trotted till they came to a river,
where they saw…

…across the water, a meadow green,
with the sweetest grass they had ever seen.

The goats longed to cross the bridge, but…

a wicked old troll lived underneath,
with horrible claws and terrible teeth,
and he gobbled up anyone trying to cross.

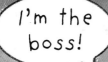

I'm the boss!

Soon the littlest billy goat Gruff said, "I'm off across the bridge to eat that sweet grass!"

And off he trotted with a trip trap, trip trap, across the wooden planks.

The wicked old troll sharpened his claws and gnashed his teeth, and…

…UP he popped with a monstrous growl!

"WHO'S THAT TRIP-TRAPPING ACROSS MY BRIDGE?"

"It's only me," said the littlest billy goat Gruff. "Please let me past, to eat the green grass!"

But the troll growled, "No! No! I'M going to eat YOU instead!"

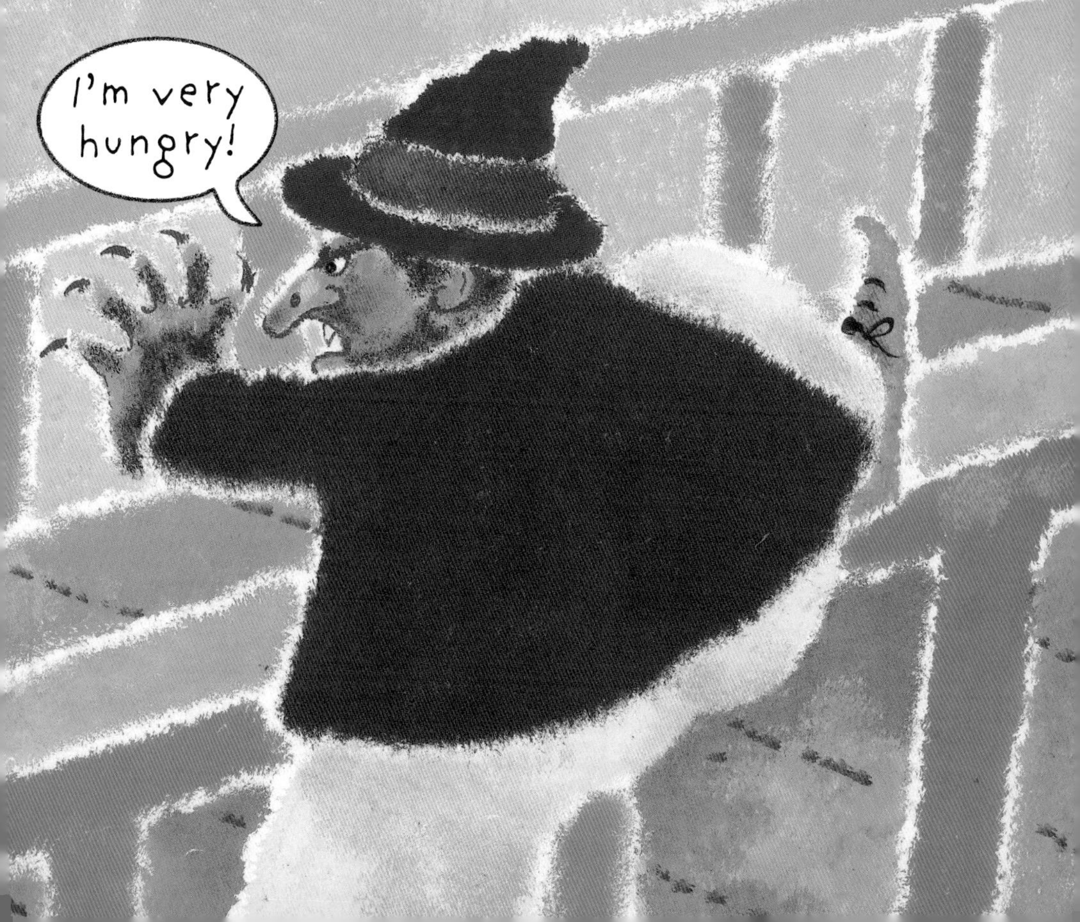

"Oh, please don't!" said the small billy goat. "Just wait a while! The second billy goat will make you smile! He's much, much bigger and fatter than I!"

And the troll thought, "Mmmmm… that's worth a try!"

So the littlest billy goat Gruff skipped over the bridge and into the meadow.

Soon the middle-sized billy goat Gruff said,
"I'm off across the bridge to eat that
sweet grass!"

And off he trotted with a trip trap, trip trap,
across the wooden planks.

The wicked old troll sharpened his claws and gnashed his teeth, and…

…UP he popped with a deafening roar!

"WHO'S THAT TRIP-TRAPPING ACROSS MY BRIDGE?"

"It's only me," said the middle-sized billy goat Gruff. "Please let me past, to eat the green grass!"

But the troll roared, "No! No! I'M going to eat YOU instead!"

"Oh, please don't!" said the middle-sized billy goat. "Just wait a while! The third billy goat will make you smile! He's much, much bigger and fatter than I!"

And the troll thought, "Mmmmm… that's worth a try!"

So the middle-sized billy goat Gruff skipped over the bridge and into the meadow.

Soon the big billy goat Gruff said,
"I'm off across the bridge to eat that
sweet grass!"

And off he trotted with a trip trap, trip trap,
across the wooden planks.

The wicked old troll sharpened his claws
and gnashed his teeth, and…

…UP he popped with a fearful holler!

"WHO'S THAT TRIP-TRAPPING ACROSS MY BRIDGE?"

"It's ME!" said the big billy goat Gruff. "I'm going past to eat the green grass!"

But the troll hollered, "No! No! I'M going to eat YOU instead!"

I'M going to eat YOU!

And the third billy goat said, in a voice like thunder…

"OH NO, YOU'RE NOT!"

Down went the billy goat's head…

...SPLASH!

into the river, never to be seen again!

Then the big billy goat Gruff skipped across the bridge to join his brothers.

And the three billy goats munched happily in pastures new, saying, "Mmmmm… this grass is so good to chew!"

MUNCH!

MUNCH!

MUNCH!